This Storybook Belongs to:
Olivia + Kaya

Princess Olivia and Kaya Kesdioler

THE LITTLE MERMAID

Two of a Kind

Enchanted Moments

ADVANCE
PUBLISHERS

Sebastian the crab was in a flurry of activity. King Triton's birthday was fast approaching and, as court composer, Sebastian was in charge of putting on a concert in the King's honor.

The little crab had just assigned everyone to an instrument or a singing part when a new mermaid arrived to join the orchestra. Sebastian wasted no time in introducing her to King Triton's daughter, Ariel, and her friend Flounder the fish.

"This is Coral," Sebastian told them. "Do you think you could look after her for a bit?" The court composer needed some time to review his music and decide where to put Coral in the performance before the next rehearsal.

"Don't worry. I'll take good care of her," replied Ariel.

"That's a pretty outfit, Coral," said Ariel. "It's unusual to see a mermaid wearing clothes, though."

Coral blushed. "Thank you. I made them myself out of seaweed. I like wearing clothes."

"And why is that?" asked Ariel, though she thought she knew the answer already.

Coral's face lit up. "That's what people wear! I've seen them."

"I know," Ariel replied. "I've been up to the surface, too!"

"You have?" Coral said in disbelief. "I thought I was the only one!"

"I know a place you'd love to see," Ariel told her.

"Shouldn't we wait here for Sebastian?" asked Coral.

"Oh, no," Ariel assured her, "rehearsal isn't for hours yet."

As the newfound friends swam through Atlantica, Ariel introduced Coral to the other merpeople they met along the way. Everyone was polite, but after Ariel and Coral passed by, many of them murmured, "*What* was she *wearing?*"

"Here it is!" announced Ariel as she, Coral, and Flounder swam into her special grotto.

Coral looked around at the shiny array of treasures that were tucked into every nook and cranny. "They're beautiful!" she gasped. "What are they?"

"Human things," said Ariel. "I've been collecting them ever since I can remember. Sometimes I find them floating on the surface of the water. And other times I find them in sunken ships."

Ariel turned to her new friend with an excited smile. "In fact, there's one ship I haven't had a chance to explore yet. Shall we go together?"

Flounder looked alarmed. "The last sunken ship had a shark in it," he reminded Ariel.

"A shark?!" cried Coral. "Maybe I'll just stay here."

"You're such a guppy!" Ariel good-naturedly scolded Flounder. "Come on, it will be fun!"

Before Coral could protest, Ariel grabbed her by the hand and led her out of the grotto. Not wanting to be left behind, Flounder reluctantly followed.

When they reached the ship, Flounder helped Coral squeeze through the porthole.

"Let the treasure hunt begin!" Ariel announced.

Coral didn't have to look very far. She spotted something she wanted right away!

"Isn't it lovely?" asked Coral, holding up the fancy pink cloth.

"It sure is," agreed Flounder. "What is it?"

"I think it's something to wear," answered Coral. "What do you think, Ariel?"

"I think we'd better go ask Scuttle," Ariel replied. "He'll know for sure. He knows all about humans."

Up to the surface they swam, where they discovered Scuttle sunning himself on a rock.

"This here," began Scuttle with authority, "is a nifty invention humans use to clean the decks of their ships. All you do is put this little number on, step into a bucket of water to get the bottom wet, then walk back and forth across the deck. Then—presto!—the ship is clean as a whistle. "

Coral wanted to stay and talk to Scuttle some more, but it was time for rehearsal. By this time, Sebastian had decided what Coral would do in the concert.

"Just bang these together when I give you the cue," instructed Sebastian as he handed her a pair of cymbals.

The orchestra began to play, and Sebastian pointed his conductor's baton at Coral. But instead of bringing the cymbals together, she dropped one of them.

Sebastian looked annoyed. "Let's try it again, from the top," he told the orchestra.

Once again, a cymbal slipped from her grasp.

"Ariel, will you *please* help our new musician?" Sebastian huffed.

"I'm sorry," Coral said. "I'm kind of clumsy."

"Just relax," Ariel told her. "Now, pretend I'm Sebastian."
She waved her arms as if conducting an imaginary orchestra.
Then she looked at Coral and pointed. Coral picked up her cymbals,
brought them together—and let them fall!

Ariel gave a weak smile. "Well, at least you played them before you dropped
them this time," she said.

Coral took her place back among the orchestra.

"I can do this," she whispered to herself.

This time, when Sebastian gave Coral her cue, she held on tightly to her cymbals and banged them against each other with a resounding CRASH!

Ariel applauded.

Coral smiled broadly and gave a bow.

"Oh, no," thought Ariel as she watched Coral fall forward onto a drum.

"'Dis is a disaster," moaned Sebastian. "Coral, I know you mean well, child, but I can't have instruments—or musicians—flying all over the stage. I'm not sure my orchestra is the place for you."

Coral's face fell. "You mean I can't be in the concert?" she asked.

Ariel spoke up before the Sebastian could answer. "Of course you can!" she said.

"Coral," the Little Mermaid continued, "you and I are alike in so many ways, I'm betting that we have something else in common, too."

"What's that?" Coral asked.

Ariel and Sebastian looked at each other and smiled. "Singing!" they cried.

Before Coral could say a word, Sebastian added, "Then it's all settled! Coral, you will sing a solo in the concert tomorrow!"

While Sebastian rehearsed the rest of the orchestra, Ariel went off to help Coral with her song. First, they decided Coral needed something fancy to wear for her performance. They agreed that the dress Coral had found earlier was perfect.

"You look beautiful," said Ariel, "now, let's hear what you sound like. Listen to what I sing, then sing it back to me, okay?"

"Okay," Coral said eagerly.

Ariel sang a verse of one of her favorite songs. Coral listened, then tried to copy the sound of Ariel's voice exactly.

"I can tell you have a lovely voice," said Ariel. "Just remember to relax and be yourself. Sing from your heart, and you will never go wrong."

The next night at the concert, Ariel sat with King Triton in the royal box. The Little Mermaid could hardly sit still waiting for Coral's solo performance.

Finally, the moment came. Coral swam to the center of the stage, took a deep breath, and sang in a voice sweet and clear. When her song was done, the audience burst into applause.

Coral looked straight up at Ariel, who gave her a wink and a broad smile. "Encore!" shouted the crowd.

When Coral looked confused, Sebastian said, "That means they want you to sing again!"

"Congratulations!" Ariel told Coral after
the show. "You were amazing! I think you have
a lot more solos in your future."

"Thank you!" said Coral. "But I have an even
better idea. Do you think we could sing a duet sometime?"

"I'd love it!" exclaimed Ariel.

Meanwhile, Sebastian was basking in the success of his concert. "King Triton said that Coral's singing was almost as lovely as Ariel's," Sebastian bragged to Flounder.

"I guess it's a good thing you didn't throw her out of the concert, huh, Sebastian?" the fish replied.

"What are you talking about?" the conductor blustered. "I knew that girl would be a star the minute I laid eyes on her!"